Chi's Sweet Home

チーズ スイート・ホーム

9

Konami Kanata

WITHDRAWN

contents

homemade 147~164+

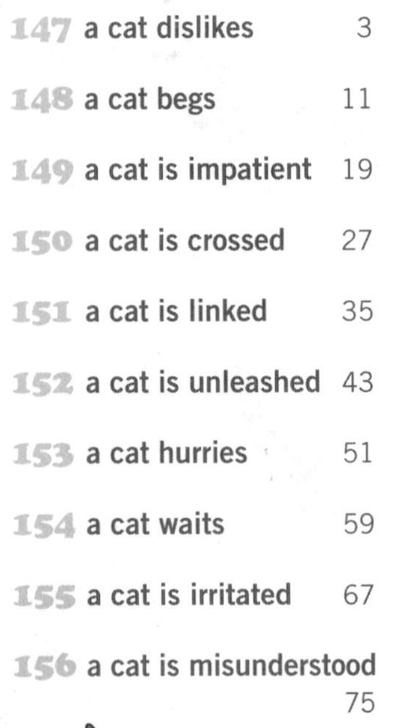

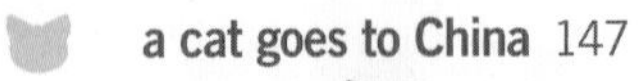

homemade 147: a cat dislikes

THE OUTDOORS...

CHI HASN'T THE CONFIDENCE TO GO OUTDOORS...

SLUMP
SIGH~

...TUNK TUNK TUNK
ZZZZ FFF

I GET SNAGGED IF I FACE DOWN.
ZHUF

RAISE

HEADS UP.
HEADS UP.
TMP TMP TMP

TMP TMP TMP
MYA
I'LL GO FLOP ON THE CUSHY-CUSH.

GLOM

MYA
SNAGGED AGAIN!

OH...

HEADS UP... HEADS UP!
RISE

PUFF
WOW!

MEOW
HOORAY! I CLIMBED IT!

AH!

TMP TMP TMP
RISE
TZCH
MEOW
CHI'S GONNA CWIMB.
HOP HOP HOP
GOING UP!
MEOW
GOING DOWN!
MEOW
HOP HOP HOP
MEOW
CHI FEELS LIKE SHE CAN DO ANYTHING!
MYA
OH, RIGHT!
PLOP
TMP TMP
TMP TMP TMP TMP TMP

RISE
KLUMP
HRN?
WHAT'S GOING ON?
HMM?
CHI'S LOOKING FUNNY.
TMP
TMP

KRUNCH
KRUNCH
KRUNCH
KRUNCH
KRUNCH
KRUNCH

KRUNCH
KRUNCH
KRUNCH

SHE'S EATING ON HER OWN NOW!
AMAZING CHI!
PFT
HOW CUTE!

WHUP

MEOW
I ATE!
MEOW
I DID IT!
MEOW
HOORAY!
TMP TMP TMP TMP
ROLL
ROLL
MEOW
I CAN DO IT!
MEOW
CHI CAN DO IT!
ROLL
ROLL
AH!
MYA
RIGHT!
WHUP
MEOW
CHI'S GOTTA GO PLAY!
DASH—

BWA—M
MEOWN

I'M STUCK!

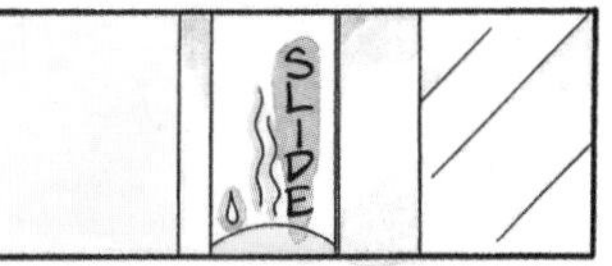
SLIDE

MYAA
OOPS!

DON'T FORGET.
MYA
HUP

GRIN

MIYA
HEADS UP! HEADS UP!
RISE

MEOW
HEAD UP AND ...

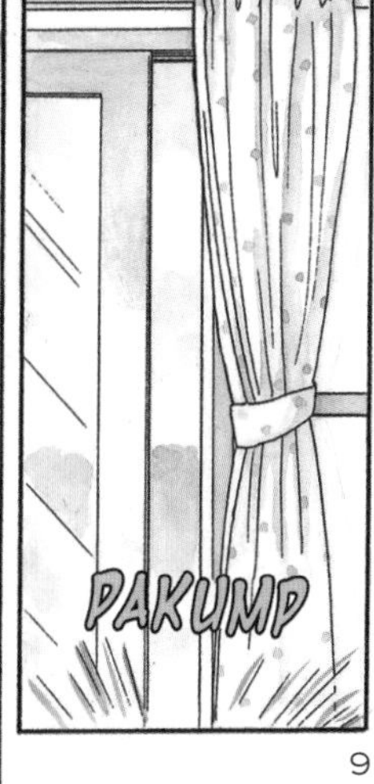
PAKUMP

HUH?
...
TURN
PRETTY INCONVENIENT, HUH.
THERE'S SO MUCH SHE CAN AND CANNOT DO.
MEOW
DADDY, OPEN THIS!
MEOW
TAKE THIS OFF!
MEOW
OPEN THIS UP!
LET'S TAKE HER TO THE VET TOMORROW.
THEY MIGHT REMOVE HER COLLAR.

the end

homemade 148: a cat begs

WE SHOULD RAISE CHI AS AN INDOOR CAT.
TURN
MEOW
CHI'S GOING OUT TO PLAY!
TMP TMP TMP
SPRING
OH, SHE'S OUT!
AH!
WAIT, WAIT, CHI!
THMP THMP
SNATCH
PHEW
MYA?
WHAT'S WRONG, DADDY?

HUH ?!
THUMP THUMP
!
MEOW
CHI'S HEADING OUT!
NUDGE NUDGE
SHUT

I DON'T GET THIS, DADDY.

BUT CHI'S GOING OUT STILL.

I KNOW HOW TO OPEN THIS.
PANG

GRIP

SKWEE
HEY?
MIYA

CHI SEEMS TO BE TRYING TO OPEN THE GLASS DOOR.
IT WON'T WORK LIKE A MESH SCREEN.

MEOW
IT'S TOO SLICK, I CAN'T GRIP IT.
SKEE
SKEE
SKEE
SKEE

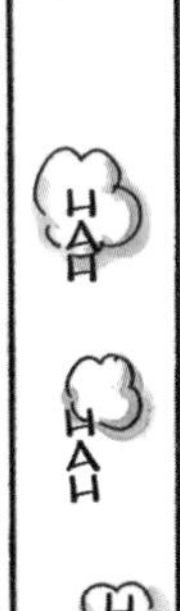
HAH
HAH
HA

HA

HOW DO I OPEN IT ?

!

YOHEY, YOHEY —
MEOW
MEOW
OPEN THIS FOR ME!

MEOW
CHI'S GOING OUT TO PLAY.

WANNA PLAY, CHI?
MEOW
OPEN IT!

HERE GOES, CHI!

TOSS
WHAT ?!

BOIN
BOIN
BOIN
BOIN

MEOW
HEY, WAIT UP! WAIT!
BOIN
BOIN
DASH—..
MYA
GOTCHA!
BOUND

HERE GOES, CHI!

HUH

YAY, I CAUGHT IT!
MEOW
KICK KICK KICK KICK

NOW HOW DO I OPEN THIS?

NO WAY.

MOMMY, OPEN THIS FOR ME.
MEOW
!

WANNA GO OUT?
WHAT TO DO.
REACH
STOP THAT.
MYA
WHY THE HAND?
OUT THERE'S NO GOOD.
MEOW
CHI'S GOING TO THE PARK.
UNDER-STAND?
MEOW
OPEN THE DOOR, MOM-MY.
PAT PAT
GOOD GIRL.
HUH?
HEY?!
THMP THMP

HOLD ON!

STICK

CHI'S GOTTA GO PLAY.
I'M SURE HE'S WAITING.
I'M SURE.
I KNOW COCCHI'S WAITING FOR ME.
MIYA MIYA
OPEN UP! OPEN UP!
MIYA MIYA
OPEN THIS UP!
SKFF SKFF SKFF SKFF
SKFF SKFF
MIYA MIYA
SOMEONE OPEN THIS!
...
MIYA MIYA MIYA
SOMEONE, ANYONE, OPEN THIS!

the end

homemade 149: a cat is impatient

FLAP
FLAP...
MRR
OH

CHIRP
CHIRP
CHIRP
MRR
HOW ABOUT WE PLAY "PINCER" ON THAT BIRD?
CHIRP
CHIRP

LEER

MIGHT BE TOO SOPHIS-TICATED FOR THAT ONE, THOUGH.

AWW
MRR

MRR
I'M CERTAIN CHI WOULD PLAY WITH A SINGLE LEAF.

YEAAAAH

MRR
CHI'S A SIMPLE ONE.
FWAP
FWAP
FWAP
FWAP

SNAP

LICK
LICK
LICK
LICK

ACTUALLY...

LEAN

DASH—...

WE DON'T EVEN NEED ANYTHING!
MRR

LOPE
LOPE

TWEET
TWEET

SPLISH

SPLUSH

YAWN

HOW LONG DOES CHI THINK I'LL WAIT?

OR MAYBE SHE'S WAITING FOR ME SOMEWHERE ELSE?

LOAF
LOAF
LOAF
LOAF
LOAF
LOAF
LOAF
LOAF
LOAF
...
HUMPH
GURG

GROWL
FLIK FLIK FLIK
MRR
I'M HUNGRY.

STAND

MRR
THERE'S NO WAY I'D WAIT FOREVER HERE.
MRR
I'M LEAVING FOR A BIT.
TP TP TP TP

TP TP TP

WOULD SHE ARRIVE WHILE I'M GONE?

LOAF LOAF LOAF LOAF

LOAF LOAF LOAF LOAF

TP
TP
TP
TP
LET'S PLAY AGAIN TOMORROW, COCCHI!
MEOW

...

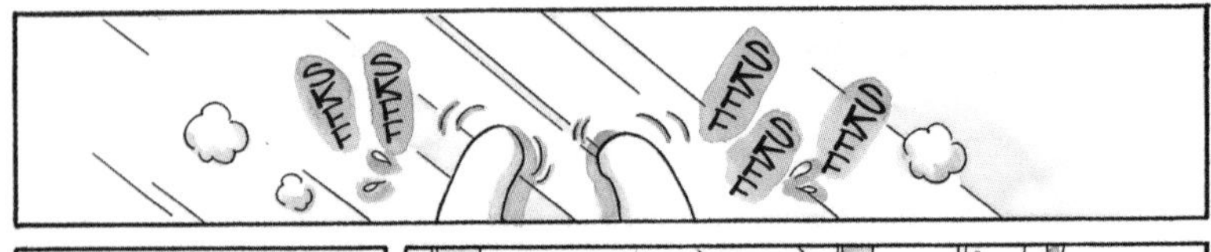
SKFF
SKFF
SKTTT
SKTTT
SKTTT

HUF
HUF
HUF
HA

MEOW
OPEN UP! OPEN UP!
SKFF
SKFF
SKTTT
SKTTT
MEOW
I'M GONNA GO PLAY!
SKFF
SKFF
SKFF

the end

homemade 150: a cat is crossed
CHI APPEARS TO HAVE FINALLY CALMED DOWN.
SHE REALLY WANTS TO GO OUT, SO IT'S A LITTLE SAD SHE CAN'T, THOUGH...
IT'S FOR HER SAFETY!

IS COCCHI STILL WAITING?

DART

MRR
I WANTED TO GO PLAY!
SCAMPER
SCAMPER
MRR
COCCHI'S WAITING FOR ME!

DASH—

FLUTT

MYA
AH!

MYA
I'VE FOUND SOME-THING NICE!
HOP

HOP
MEOW
YAY, I'VE CAUGHT IT!
GRAB
WHIP
WHIP

MEOW MEOW
YAY YAY
MEOW
SO MUCH FUN!
KICK
KICK
KICK

SNAP

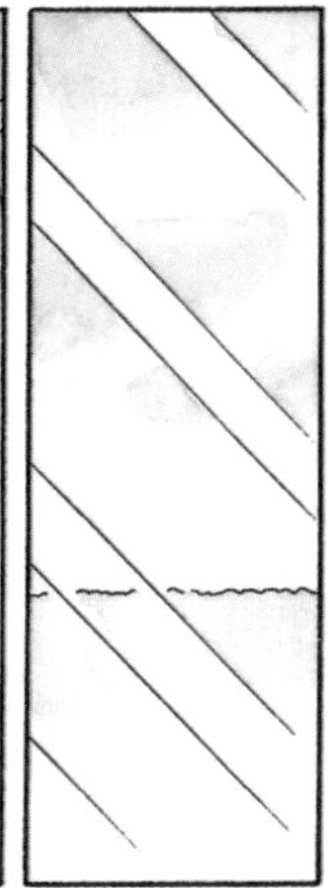

I WONDER WHAT COCCHI'S UP TO?

MEOW
AND CHI PROMISED!
BOUND

KICK KICK KICK KICK
CHI DID!
MIYA

GNAW GNAW GNAW
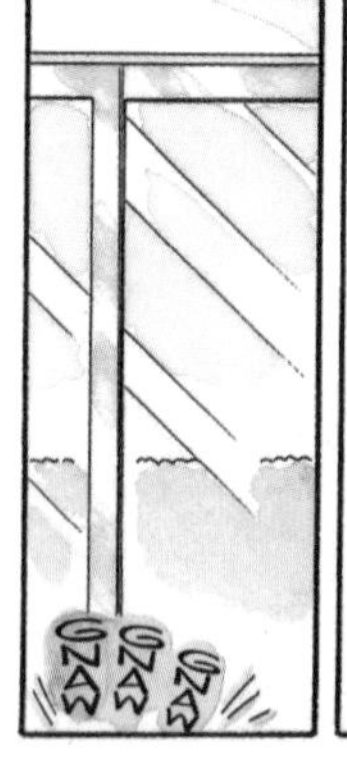
GNAW GNAW GNAW

DINNER TIME!
CHI, DINNER.
CHI.

CHI
STEAMED

!
YOINK

MEOW
CHI DOESN'T NEED ANY FOOD.
KICK
KICK
KICK

...

I'LL JUST HAVE A BITE.

BITE

WANNA TRY THIS, CHI?

MYA!
WOW!

GRIP
MEOW
YAY, GIMME!

MEOW
SO TASTY! YUM!
CHEW CHEW
WANT SOME MORE?

MEOW
HOORAY!
MEOW
CHI'S EATING LOTS!
MUNCH MUNCH MUNCH

MEOW
I'M ALL FULL.
HA

OH!

LATER, COCCHI!

SEE YOU TOMORROW!

the end

homemade 151: a cat is linked

TIP
TIP
TIP
TIP
NO, CHI, YOU CAN'T GO OUT.
BAM
BAD !
OKAY, LET'S GO.
SAY,
IF CHI ...

CAN'T GO OUT, THEN SHE'LL BE LONELY, RIGHT?

...

TURN

TIP
TIP

IT SURE IS SAD TO NOT HAVE HER GO OUT.

IT'S SO DANGEROUS OUT THERE.
IT WOULD BE SO MUCH SAFER TO JUST RAISE HER AS AN INDOOR CAT.
BUT
BEING OUTDOORS HAS BEEN PART OF HER LIFE.
BUT
FUSS
FUSS

IT'S A SHAME.
BUT
I WORRY.
BUT STILL ...
HOWEVER...
FUSS
FUSS
FUSS

WHAT TO DO !
SCRATCH
SCRATCH

LET'S GO, DAVID!
RUFF RUFF

RUFF RUFF

BOUND
WHUM

SKIP SKIP
RUFF
RUFF
OH
HEL-
LO!
DAVID, GO!
RUFF RUFF
TAP TAP TAP
THAT'S
IT!

TO THE PET SHOP! GO!
BWA HA.

WHAT'S THAT?
CAN IT BE?

SHOOM
PET SHOP

MEOW
KSH
KSH
PET SHOP
KSH

IT'S A LEASH!

TO ATTACH TO HER COLLAR.

THIS WAY WE CAN TAKE CHI OUTDOORS.
YOU MEAN, YOU PLAN TO WALK CHI?
JUST LIKE DAVID NEXT DOOR?
RIGHT!
KSH
KSH
PET SHOP

SHI-K
MEOW

LET'S PUT HER COLLAR ON...
KLIK
THEN WE HOOK ON THE LEASH.
SWIP SWIP

SWIP
SWIP

FROM NOW ON...
SWIP SWIP

CHI, COME ALONG!
MEOWN MEOWN MEOWN

I CAN HAVE A FUN WALK WITH CHI!

KLAK

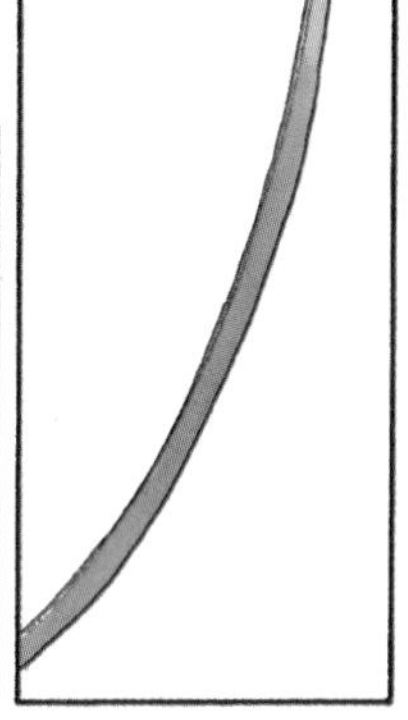

the end

homemade 152: a cat is unleashed

WE'RE OFF!
YAY
MEOW
DART
MEOW
I'M OFF TO THE PARK!

SNAP

HUH?
GAG?!

OH

RIGHT ...

COME ALONG, CHI.
THIS WAY.

THIS IS STUCK ON ME.

TUG
TUG

TWING
TWING

BING
BING

I'M STUCK. STUCK!

WHAT'S WRONG, CHI?
...

SOME-THING'S WRONG.

RIGHT! OKAY.
YOU WANT TO GO THAT WAY THEN.
STEP-STEP...

LET'S GO!
TUG

YANK
!
BALK

GRIP

LET'S GO WALKING, CHI.

MEOW
WHAT ARE YOU THINKING, DADDY?

RIGHT, THIS IS YOUR FIRST WALK.
SEE, WE'RE GOING WALKING TOGETHER...
THIS WAY.
STEP STEP
AND—

IT'S OKAY, YOU LEAD.
COME ON.
TIP TIP TIP

HUH ?

OK,
LET'S GO, CHI!

!
BALK

BRACE

COME ON, CHI.
TUG TUG

HRN~

COME ON ...
TUG TUG

STRUT STRUT STRUT STRUT

CHI
STRUT
STRUT
STRUT
WHAT ARE YA DOING?
MEOW
COME ALONG NOW, CHI!
CHI—
STOP IT!
MEOW
WHAP
WHAP
WHAP
MIYA
NO WAY!
WHUM
POP
HUH?
MYA?
OH

WOAH!

MEOW!
CHI'S GOING TO THE PARK NOW!
DASH

HEY, CHI!
DASH—

CHI, WAIT!

MEOW
I'LL BE BACK, DADDY!
HOP

CHI!

DASH—

...

SPLISH
SPLISH
LOAF
LOAF
LOAF
LOAF

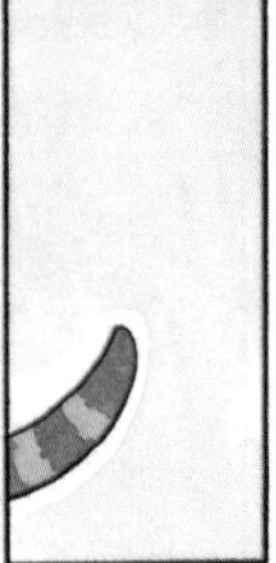

MRRR?!

CHI?!

I'M JUST A LITTLE LATE...
HUE
HUE

GRIN

I'M ON MY WAY NOW, COCCHI.
MEOW
HA
HUE
HA

the end

homemade 153: a cat hurries

MEOW
I'M COMING!
COCCHI'S WAITING.
MEOW
DASH
MEOW
WHAT WILL WE PLAY?
GRIN
SPLISH!
STEAMED

HOP
TSK
MRR
MRR
WELL, I AIN'T WAITING ANY LONGER.
TIPTIP TIP

MEOWN
SKIP

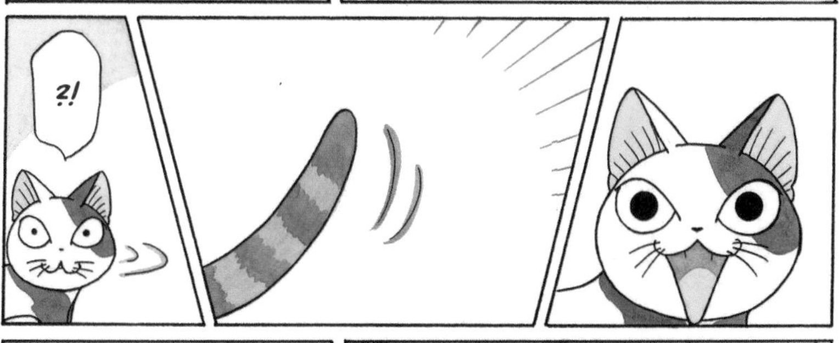
?!

IT'S CHI!

MRR
CHI, I'M OVER HERE!
HOP
YO, CHI!
MRR

MRR
HEY? WHERE'D CHI GO?
PEER PEER

SKIP

TMP
MRR
THERE SHE IS!

RIGHT!
I'LL SNEAK UP AND SURPRISE HER.

SCUTTLE
BOUND

MRR
I'M OVER HERE!
BOUND

MRR
YO, TAKE THIS, CHI!

CLUTCH

MEOWR
MOMMA!
HUH?

WHAT?

MEOWN
WHAT ARE YOU DOING?
MRR
CHI?

HAH
HAH
SPLISH!

HUFF
HEY?

SPLISH
MEOW
WHERE'S COCCHI?

MIYA
COCCHI COĈCHI
SAUNT SAUNT

SAUNT SAUNT
MIYA
CHI'S HERE!

MEOW
WHERE ARE YOU, COCCHI?

MRRR!
THAT'S NOT CHI!
HUH?
NYAR
WHAT YOU DOING TO MY KITTEN?
SPLUSH
MYA
COCCHI'S NOT HERE.

the end

homemade 154: a cat waits

WHO ARE THEY?

THAT ONE LOOKS JUST LIKE CHI.

SLINK SLINK

SHE WAS LOCKED IN WHEN SHE WANTED TO GO OUT,

AND SHE MIGHT BE AGAIN IF SHE RETURNS.

IS SHE GOING TO COME BACK?

SHE WENT THAT WAY, RIGHT?
YEAH
LET'S GO SEARCHING THAT WAY.
CHI
CHI
CHI
CHI
RESTAURANT
Park Side
CHI
WHERE ARE YOU, CHI?
COME, CHI!
CHI
RUFF
OH!

HELLO
RUFF RUFF

OH, KUSANO FROM NEXT DOOR.
A WALK, HUH?
YES
WHAT'S THE MATTER?
DAVID!
RUFF

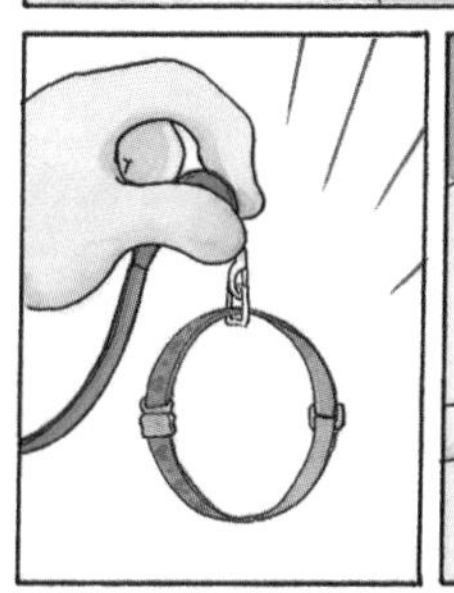

WE'RE LOOKING FOR CHI...

SNIFF
SNIFF
SNIFF

DAVID?
RUFF
SNIFF SNIFF

SNIFF SNIFF
SNIFF SNIFF
DOES HE KNOW CHI'S SCENT?
YOU'RE AMAZING, DAVID!
HE'S ONLY A NORMAL DOG.
SNIFF SNIFF
SNIFF SNIFF
PLEASE HELP US, DAVID.

YO.
NYO
IT'S BLACKIE!
MEOW

ARE YOU HERE ALONE?
NYO
MEOW
HEY, HAVE YOU SEEN COCCHI?
I HAVE A PROMISE WITH COCCHI.
MEOW
AND CHI'S FINALLY HERE.
MEOW
NYO
I HAVEN'T SEEN HIM TODAY.
MEOW
NYO
WELL THEN...
WAIT, WAIT!
SKAMPER
MEOW
IF YOU SEE COCCHI, TELL HIM!
OH, IT'S THE PARK.
GREEN PARK
SNIFF
SNIFF
SNIFF
SNIFF
RUFF!
OH?!
IS SHE HERE?

RUFF
RUFF
THAT WAY!
RUFF
DAA———SH
SPRING
RUFF
RUFF
HM?!
YAKITOR
MEOW
TELL HIM, "CHI IS WAITING."
NYO
OKAY.

the end

homemade 155: a cat is irritated

MEOW
CHI'S WAITING!
SOAR SOAR SOAR
MEOW
ARE YOU IN HERE?
PEEK
MEOW
COCCHI
MEOW
HEY!
MEOW
CHI'S BEEN WAITING FOREVER.
SAUNT SAUNT SAUNT
SIGH~

MEOW
WHEN WILL COCCHI GET HERE?

VWSH

CAW CAW

HOW LONG SHOULD CHI WAIT?

CAW
THE SUN WILL GO AWAY...
AND IT'LL BE NIGHT.

IT'LL GET DARK,
I WAIT,
UNTIL IT'S ALL DARK,
AND I'LL BE HUNGRY
THEN IT'LL GET EVEN DARKER...

GLOOM
MEOWN
CHI'S NOT GONNA WAIT THAT LONG.
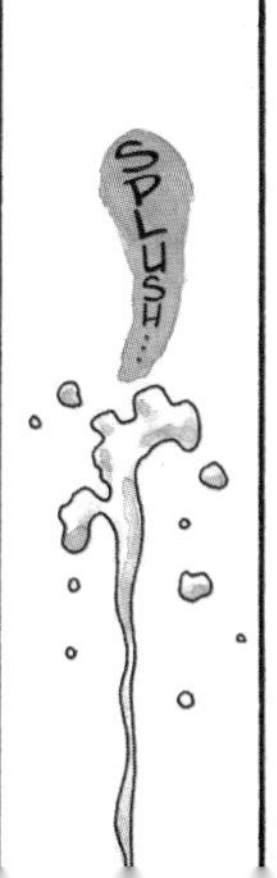
SPLUSH...

PLIP

OR,
WHAT IF...

HE NEVER INTENDED TO COME AT ALL.

KRRRR

MEOW
COCCHI, THAT PUNK!
KRRRR

KRRRR
KRRRR
OH, IT'S THE LITTLE ONE.
NYA

NYA
IT'S ABOUT TIME TO GO HOME.

MYA
AUNTIE CALICO.
NYA
IT'S TIME FOR THE SUN TO SET.

NYA
TYKES SHOULD GO HOME AND DRINK THEIR MILKS.

MIYA
YOU ARE RIGHT.
SPR-ING

MEOW
CHI'S GOING HOME.

MEOW
I'M SURE COCCHI'S AT HOME.
SNORT SNORT

LAP LAP LAP
SNUG SNUG

WE PROM-ISED!
MEOW
KRRR

YOU DON'T CARE ABOUT ME?
MEOW
KRRR

CHI CAME AFTER ALL!
MEOW
KRRR

MEOW
THAT COCCHI... HRMPH!

NYA
THAT ONE DOESN'T HAVE A "HOME."

MYA?
HUH?

NYA
HE DOESN'T HAVE A HOME LIKE YOU.
MYA?
HUH?
NYA
THAT'S BECAUSE HE'S A STRAY.
MYA?
WHAT?

HE LIVES ALONE.
NYA
HE BASICALLY WANDERS ABOUT.
NYA...
AND YET...

I THINK HE WAS HERE ALL AFTERNOON.
OH?
SO THEN...

the end

homemade 156: a cat is misunderstood
SNEAK SNEAK
SNEAK SNEAK
SNEAK SNEAK
SNEAK

YOU SURE DO LOOK LIKE CHI.

SO THERE ARE OTHERS THAT LOOK LIKE CHI, HUH?

NYAN
NOW GO ON HOME.

"HOME"
?

TIP TIP

HUH.
SO THOSE GUYS HAVE A HOME, TOO.

...

FWIP
OOPS!

WHAT THE?

WHAT IS SHE LOOKING FOR?

NYAO

NYAO
NYAO
NYAO
NYAON
WHO WAS THAT CAT CALLING?

SHE WAS LOOKING
FOR SOMEONE.

MRR
TSK, MORE IMPOR-TANTLY ...

I NEVER GOT TO MEET CHI.

IS SHE "HOME," TOO?
MEOW
MEOW

MRR
I GUESS I'LL PASS ON BY THEN.

CHI WASN'T OVER THERE AFTER ALL.
DO WE LOOK MORE?
IT'S OKAY.

I'M SURE SHE'LL COME BACK HOME.
SHE ALWAYS HAS BEFORE.

PLOP

MRR
ARE YOU THERE, CHI?
MRR
CHI

THE COCCHI HAS COME BY...
MRR
MRR
YO, CHI—
ZING ZING

ZING
ZING
ZING
ZING

the end

homemade 157: a cat yearns
TP
TP
TP
HA
GREEN PARK
GREEN PARK
TUP
TUP
TUP
TUP

SIGHHH

MEOW
WHAT SHOULD I DO NOW?
HOW LONG DO I WAIT?
MEOW

MYA
COCCHI'S NOT AROUND ...
MYA
AND IT'S NIGHT TIME.

OOH!
MRR
MEOW
YEAH!

MEOW
FINALLY, WE MEET!
MRR
I WAS LOOKING FOR YA!

MRR!
CHI!
MEOW!
IT'S COCCHI!

MRR
I THOUGHT YOU WERE "HOME."
MYA
I CAME.
SCAMPER

MEOW
I'M GLAD YOU'RE HERE, COCCHI.
MRR
AND YOU FINALLY GOT HERE.
SCAMPER

MEOW
YAY!
YAY!
MRR
SCAMPER
SCAMPER

HUFF
HUFF
HUFF
HUFF

HA

MEOW
I MEAN, WE JUST MET UP.
MRR
CHI BETTER NOT GO HOME.
MYA
HUH?!

MEOW
CHI'S HAD IT ROUGH.

BUT I FINALLY MADE IT.
MYA
MRR
THAT "HOME" SOUNDS LIKE A BOTHER.

MRR
ON THE OTHER HAND...
MRR
WHEREVER I GO OR WHATEVER I DO...
SWAG
SWAG
SWAG

TURN

MRR
I'M FREE!
SPARK

WOW!

MEOW
SO COOL!

MEOW
CHI SHOULD DO THAT, TOO!
MYA
HUH, WAIT ...
M MRR
WHAT? BE FREE?

YEAH, THAT!
MYA

GRIN

MEOW!
CHI'S GONNA BE FWEE!

...MYA
...SO

MEOW
HOW DO I START BEING FWEE?

MRR
WITH FOOD!

MEOW
FOOD? DINNER?!
MYA
WHERE?
MYA
WHAT?
MEOW
CHI CAN EAT A LOT!

SKRUM

MRR
WE CAN SQUEEZE IN FROM BELOW.

SHUV SHUV SHUV

MEOW
WHAT IS THIS PLACE?

PUB
ODEN
ETC.

the end

homemade 158: a cat apprentices

SHUV
SHUV
SHUV

YOU'VE GOTTA GRAB YOUR OWN FOOD!
MRR
SHUV

SKWEEN
SKWEEN
SKWEEN

MEOW
GOT IT!

MYA
YAY!
DASH

MEOW
CHI'S GONNA EAT FWEELY!

SHUV
SHUV
SHUV
SHUV
SHUV
SHUV
SHUV
SHUV

MEOW
I'VE FOUND SOME CRUNCHY FOODS!

PHA

WOW!

YOU MADE IT!
MRR

MEOW
THIS IS CHI'S FIRST TIME HAVING THIS FOOD!

MEOW
I'M DIGGING IN!

SHUV
MEOW

MEOW
WHAT ARE YOU DOING?

MEOW
NUDGE

MEOW
WHAT'S GOING ON?

SMUSH

FISK
WHAT'S GOING ON?
FISK
NO PUSHING!

FISK
CHI'S DINNER—

PUB
ODEN ETC.

HUFF
HUFF
HUFF

MRR
DID YOU GET TO EAT?

IT WAS NO GOOD ...
MYA

MYA
OH

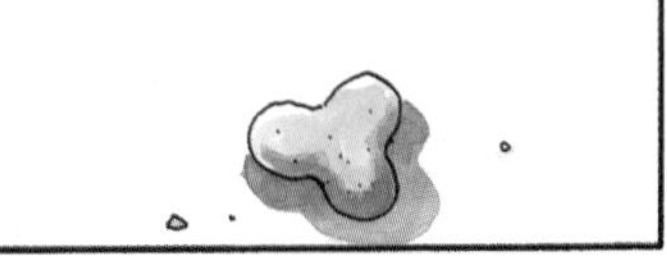

HUP
MEOW!
ONE PIECE IS LEFT!

THANKS FOR THE...
MEOI

CLUTCH
SLIDE

KRUNCH
KRUNCH

SMAK
!!!

I ALSO ONLY GOT TO EAT A BIT.
MRR
SO FRUS-TRATING!
MEOW

GRIP

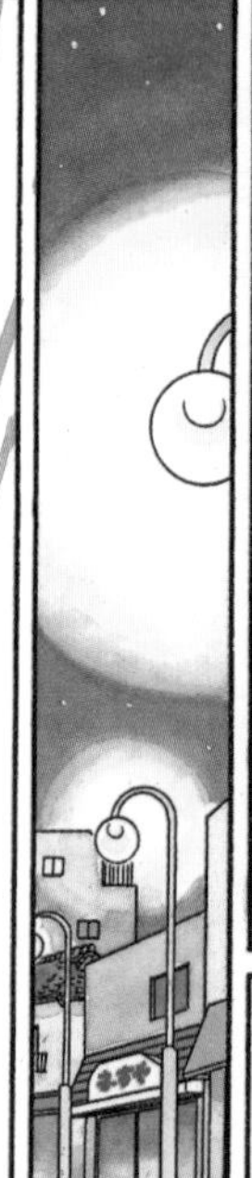

MEOW
CHI'S MORTI-FIED!

MRR
I WANNA BE STRONG!
SKSH
MRR
I CAN'T WAIT TO GROW BIGGER!
SKSH SKSH
SKSH

SKSH

SKSH SKSH
MEOW
CHI WANTS TO GET BIGGER, TOO.
SKSH SKSH

MEOW
I WANNA BE AS BIG AS YOHEY.
SKSH
YOHEY?
...AH!

MRR!
IMPOS-SIBLE!

MYA
HEY~ REALLY ?
MRR
IT'S JUST NOT POSSIBLE.
MRR
BUT

WE CATS HAVE ...
MRR
MRR
JUMPING SKILLZ AND SHARP CLAWS!

"WE CATS" ...?

MRR
LET'S GO TO THE NEXT MEAL!

WHA!
MYA

MEOW
HOORAY!
GRRR
GRRR

the end

homemade 159: a cat practices
GRRRR
MEOW
CHI'S HUNGWY.
MEOW
DINNER
MEOW
DINNER
MRR
STOP MUTTERING OVER THERE.

MYA?
HUH?
MRR
COME OVER HERE SO THEY CAN HEAR US BETTER.
MRR
YOU CAN'T SURVIVE LIKE THAT!
MYA
GOT IT.

DINNER —
MRR
MEOW
DINNER, DINNER!
MRR
LOUDER!
AYE!
MYA

GIVE US DINNER!
MRR MRR
MEOW
DINNER!
MEOW
DINNER!
MRR
KEEP IT UP, A BIT MORE!
AYE!
MYA

MEOW
DINNER
DINNER
MEOW

MEOW
MEOW
MEOW
MRR
MRR
MRR
MEOW
MRR
SLIDE

SO YOU'VE COME BACK AGAIN, LITTLE ONE.
OH, AND THERE'S ANOTHER KITTEN WITH YOU TODAY.
DINN...
MYA...
MYA...
DINN...
PANT PANT
MRR

PANT
PANT
PANT
PANT
PANT

FRUMP
HA

OH MY GOOD-NESS,
I MUST GET YOU SOME-THING.

TADAA

!

WHAT ARE THESE?
MYA
MYA
WHAT?

THEY'RE REAL TASTY!
MRR
SNIFF SNIFF

MEOW
THEY SMELL GOOD!

IT'S SOME LEFTOVER CHICKEN.
MEOW
THANKS FOR THE MEAL!
MUNCH

MUNCH MUNCH
MUNCH MUNCH
MEOW
YUM, DELISH ...

THIS FLAVOR— CHI'S...

NEVER TASTED BEFORE!
WOOOOW

MUNCH
MUNCH
MUNCH
CHEW
CHEW
CHEW
MUNCH

MORE, MORE!
MRR MRR
SMAK SMAK

GIVE US MORE!
MRR!

OKAY, THAT'S ENOUGH.
SLIDE
BYE, NOW.

...

PLUNK

HALT

HUH
?

MY
...

HMM
?
OH,

PWEASE

PWEASE

PWEASE

'KAY?
TILT

WHA ?!
CHARM
CHARM

SLIDE
MY, WHAT TO DO?

WHAT ?!

...

TILT

PWEASE ♡

MAYBE SHE CAN MAKE IT ...

the end

homemade 160: a cat is sleepy

MRR
WE'VE GOTTA GET TO THE PARK.
MRR
GOT IT?

MIYA...
SLEEPY...

MRR
WE SLEEP AT MY DEN #1!
MRR
DON'T FALL ASLEEP HERE!
SLUMP

MRR
'CAUSE SLEEPING IN THE STREET IS REALLY DANGER-OUS.
MRR
ALL RIGHT!

MIYA
UH-HUH
FLOP

...

MRR!
YOU JUST NODDED AND FELL ASLEEP!
SNAP

MRR
...
I'M SLEEPY TOO BUT I'M HANGING IN HERE.

PLUP
PLUP
PLUP

TEETER

TEETER
MRR
WOAH!
MRR
YOU'RE GONNA FALL!

MRR
YOU CAN'T SLEEP SOUNDLY IN AN UNSAFE PLACE.
...

RAISE

FLOP

TOPPLE

WHAT?
MRR
MRR
CHI!
FWUMP

MRR
DON'T FALL ASLEEP!
MRR
WAKE UP!

I DON'T LIKE THIS PLACE, BUT...

I CAN'T MOVE.

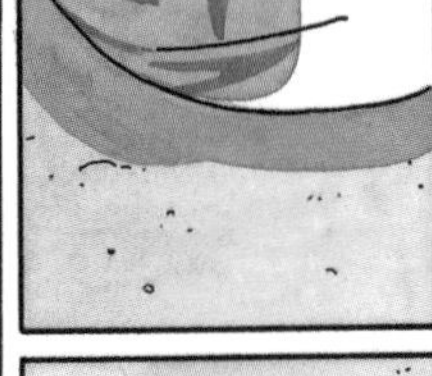

CHI'S GONNA TURN INTO THE STREET LIKE THIS.

MRR
I'M SAYING, WAKE UP!
SHUV SHUV
PUSH
SLUMP
THUNK

MRR
WOAH
MRR
WOAH
MYA
GIVE ME A BREAK~

THIS IS NICE.
OR DADDY ...
IT'S NOT MY CUSHY CUSH ...
FLOP
G'NIGHT, COCCHI...

IS IT LIKE CHI?!
IT'S NOT CHI.
THEN WHAT?
SMAK SMAK
MRR
WAKE UP, CHI!
CHI!
MRR!

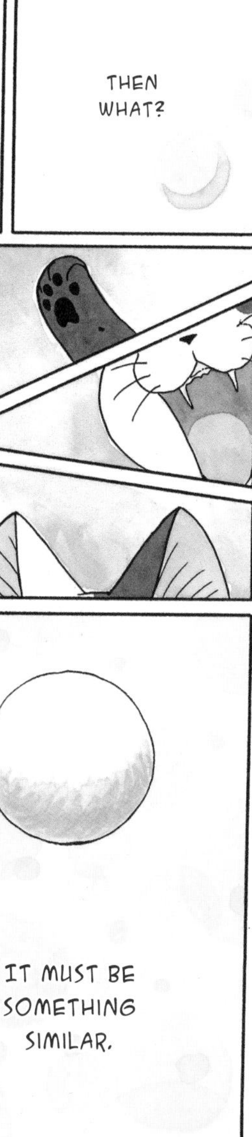
IT MUST BE SOMETHING SIMILAR.

CHI

WON'T BECOME A "STREET," BUT...

the end

homemade 161: a cat is hunted
CHI HASN'T RETURNED AT ALL, HUH.
I HOPE SHE'S OKAY.
IT'S PRETTY LATE.
STEAM
STEAM
HRN ~

...
...
...
LET'S GO LOOK FOR HER AGAIN!
LET'S SPLIT IN TWO AND SEARCH.
RIGHT
YOHEI AND I WILL GO LOOK THAT WAY.
AND I'LL GO SEARCH IN THAT DIRECTION.
I'LL CALL IF WE FIND HER!
BYE!

CHI
CHI

WHERE ARE YOU?
CHI

AH
THE PARK

FULL OF BUSHES CATS LOVE.
SO DARK AND WIDE.

CHI
CHI, ANSWER IF YOU'RE HERE!
SHAK
SHAK
SHAK
SHAK

WHERE ARE YOU?
CHI
SHAK
SHAK
SHAK

CHI

I'LL HEAD DOWN THIS WAY.

YOU THERE, CHI?
SHAK

CHI

CHI
CHI

CHI
CHI... WHERE ARE YOU?

CHI'S A LITTLE KITTY... SHE'S SO SMALL IT'S TOUGH FINDING HER.
HA

TIP
TIP TIP

HM ?

TIP TIP TIP

CHI!

I'VE FOUND HER!
COME QUICK!

YAY! WHERE AT?
YEAH!
ZASH
BOUND

WE'VE FOUND HER!
HOORAY

YAY YAY

MEW

HEY!
MEW
SWIP SWIP
CHI
CHI
THANK GOODNESS.
COME ON, STOP STRUGGLING NOW, CHI.
SWIP SWIP
CHI!
HM?

WHAT'S THE MATTER?
...
WHAT'S UP?

SHE LOOKS LIKE CHI, BUT...

HUH?

IT'S NOT CHI!

WHAT?!

MYAU
MYAU
OH?

MYAUU

DASH
MEW

THEY REALLY LOOK ALIKE, HUH?
YEAH
NOW, WHERE IS CHI?

WHAT? THAT'S NOT CHI?!

SKOOT——..

the end

homemade 162: a cat is exhausted

MRR
HEY, WAKE UP, CHI!
NUDGE NUDGE
YOU CAN'T SLEEP IN A PLACE LIKE THIS.
MRR

MUMBL MUMBL
HNNN

HOW CAN SHE BE SO CAREFREE?

OOORV
HUH?
MRR?

OOORV

OOORV

MRR
WHOA?!

MRR
COME ON, WAKE UP!
YOU'LL GET RUN OVER!
SMAR
SMAR
MRR

MRR
CHI!
SMAR SMAR
HNN
NNMEE
PLEASE STOP~

CURL

MRR
I'M SAYING YOU'RE IN DANGER! UNDER-STAND?!
MRR
CHI!
SHY
SHY
SHY
SHY

MRR
CHI, YOU DUMMY!

VROOO

VROOM

VWOOM

VRRN

HA

ZZZ

...

MRR
HEY, I'M PRETTY SLEEPY TOO, YOU KNOW!
YAWN

SNAP

MRR
I CAN'T FALL ASLEEP.
MUST NOT.
MRR
SHAKE
SHAKE
SHAKE

MRR
YOU CAN'T GO TO SLEEP HERE.
NUDGE
NUDGE
HEY, CHI!
MRR

MUMBL

MRRR
DON'T YOU FALL ASLEEP!
JOLT
JOLT
JOLT
NO SLEEPING!
MRR~

MUMBL
MUMBL
MUMBL
...

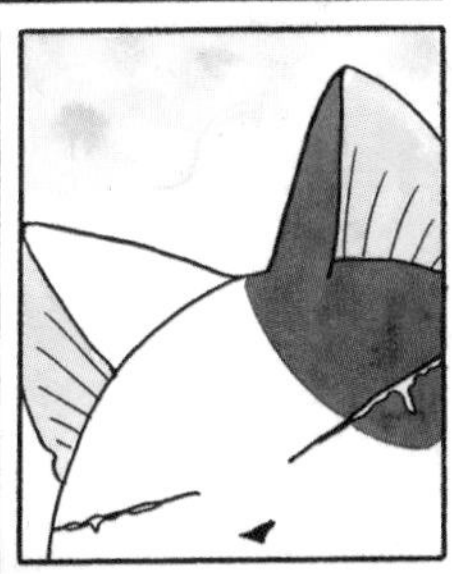

SLUMP

WHERE ARE YOU?
HEY
CHI

HMM?

IT'S SO SOFT AND WARM...

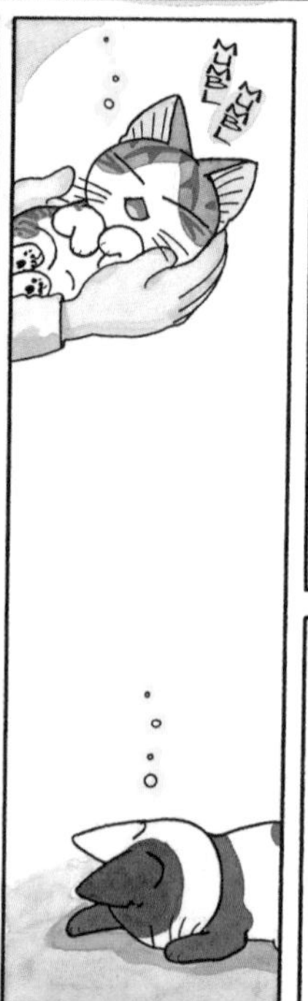
MUMBL MUMBL

OH
CHI!
AH, THANK GOODNESS!
WHAT SHOULD WE DO ABOUT THIS KITTY?

HJA HJA

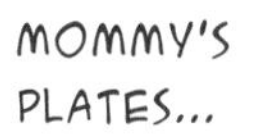

OH, THAT'S A YOHEY SOUND.

KLAK
TUNK
I'LL HAVE IT BLACK ...

MOMMY'S PLATES...
AND DADDY'S VOICE...

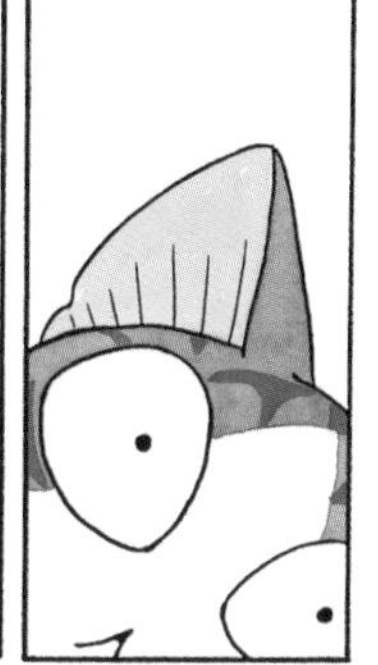

STAND

MYA?
HEY?
STAND

MRR
HUH?
MRR?!
WHAT?!
MEOW?!
SHE'S WOKEN UP CONFUSED.
AND WE COULDN'T JUST LEAVE THE OTHER KITTEN BACK THERE...
WHERE IS THIS?
MEOW?
WHY ARE WE HOME?
MRR?
MRR?
WHAT THE WHAT?

the end

homemade 163: a cat is the same as ever

THIS
...

LET'S GO HOME.
HOME
—

THIS IS "HOME."

MEOW
GRRRRR
I GUESS I'M HUNGRY.

FOOD... I BETTER GO LOOK FOR SOME.
GRRRRRR

MRR
LATER

GIVEN THE TIME...
THERE SHOULD BE FOOD AT THAT PLACE.

GRIT
I BETTER GET ON IT.

SNAKT
OH!

MEOW
YAY YAY!
IT'S FOOD!
MEOW
DASH——..

SQUAT

HMM ?

STILL

WHY'S SHE JUST SITTING STILL THERE?

HERE.
YAY!
MYA!

TURN

MEOW
IT'S BREAK-FAST, COCCHI!

MEOW
FOOD'S READY!

HUH?!

WHAT?!

MRR
YOU JUST SIT DOWN AND YOUR MEAL SHOWS UP?!

?

MYA
THAT'S RIGHT.

...

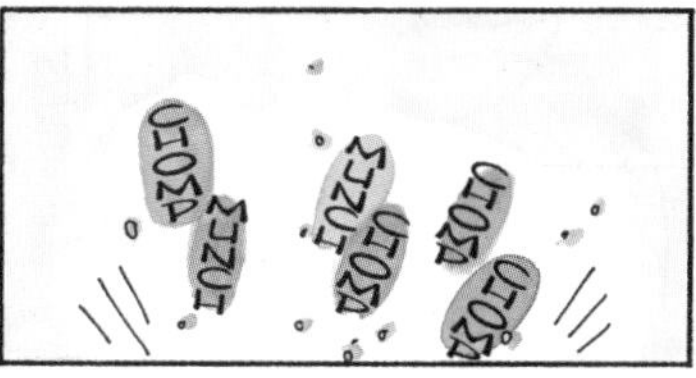
CHOMP
MUNCH
MUNCH
CHOMP
CHOMP
CHOMP

THIS IS ENTIRELY DIFFERENT FROM ME.
MRR
MRR
MUNCH
MUNCH
CHOMP
CHOMP
MUNCH

HEY, CHI—
YOU'VE LEFT A BIT.

HMM ?!

WHA
?!
CHOMP

MUNCH
MUNCH
MUNCH

THEY ACTUALLY HOLD THE PLATE FOR YOU TO EAT FROM?!
MRR?!

MEOW
I'M SHTUFFED.

WOW, WHAT A REAL LAZY LIFE.
BURP

HAA~

WHAT
?

FLOP

HUH
?

ROLL

MIYA?
ANYTHING WRONG?

HMM
?
MEE
MRR
YOU EAT AND JUST GO TO SLEEP LIKE THAT?!

MRR
YOU HAVE TO FIND A SAFE SPOT TO REST IN!
MRR
YOU'VE GOTTA FIND FOOD YOUR YOURSELF
MRR
BARING YOUR TUMMY IS DANGEROUS!
MRR
AND EAT YOUR OWN FIND!

the end

homemade 164: a cat feels at home

LICK LICK LICK

MRR
WHY ARE YOU GROOMING YOURSELF LYING DOWN?!
SLIK SLIK SLIK

MEE?
HMM ?

MYA?
DIDN'T YA KNOW, COCCHI?

YOU CAN DO IT FLOPPED DOWN.
MEOW

LICK LICK
MEOW
LOOK !

MYA~
MY BACK IS HARD TO REACH, THOUGH!

MRR
THAT'S NOT WHAT I MEAN!

MRR
WHAT IS UP WITH THIS UNGUARDED LAZINESS...

MRR
THAT TAKES THE CAKE.
LICK
LICK
LICK
LICK

SLIK
SLIK
SLIK
SLIK
SLIK

MEOW
AHHH~
HRN?

YEAH~
MIYA~

WHAT'S HE DOING?

MIYA
BRUSH-BRUSH FEELS SO GOOD...

BRUSH-BRUSH?

...

MEOWN
DADDY, MORE!

YOU GET YOUR GROOMING DONE FOR YOU?!
MRR

WHAT'S THAT?

?!
Z-ZM
FWIP FWIP
FWIP FWIP

FWIP FWIP FWIP FWIP

BWAAAH

IS IT ALIVE? MAYBE PREY?
IS IT A TAIL?
FWIP FWIP FWIP FWIP FWIP FWIP

MEOW
NICE, THEY'RE PLAYING WITH YOU!
HUH ?!

MEOW
CHI WANTS TO PLAY, TOO.
DASH——

PLAY ...
"WITH" ?

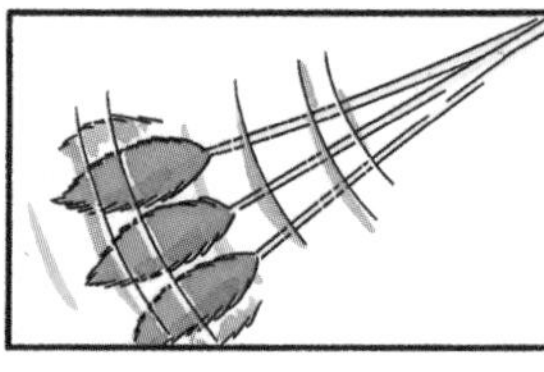

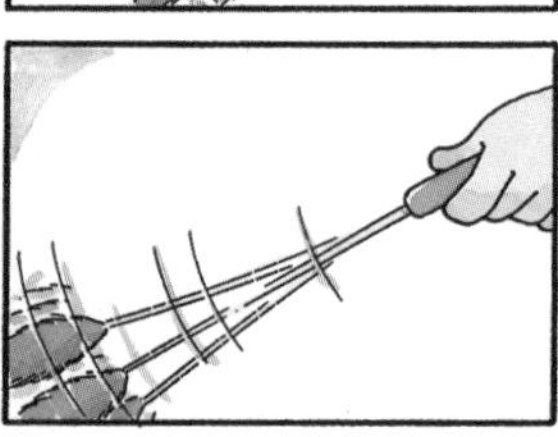

!
WOAH !
MYA

MRR
THEY PLAY WITH YOU?!

HOP
HOP

MEOW
COCCHI, COME AND PLAY!
MEOW
IT'S FUN!

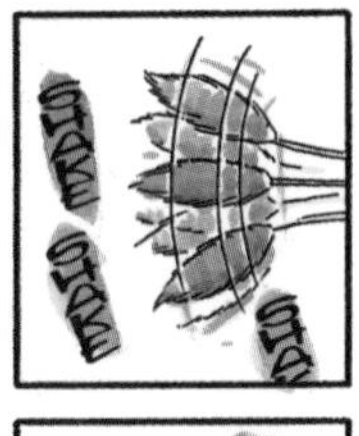
SHAKE
SHAKE

WHIP
WHIP
WHIP

FWIP
FWIP
FWIP
FWIP

FWIP
FWIP
FWIP
FWIP

MRRR
YEAH
D SH

MRR
MEOW
DART
DASH

MEOW
MRR
HOP
HOP

MEOW
FWIP FWIP
DASH
WOAH YEAH
MMM RRR RRR
DASH
MRR

HUFF

HUFF

HUFF
HUFF

THIS IS MY CUSH-CUSH.
MEOW
SNUG
SNUG

HUFF
HUFF
HUFF
HA

SMUSH
SMUSH

the end

homemade special  a cat goes to China

Chi's Sweet Home

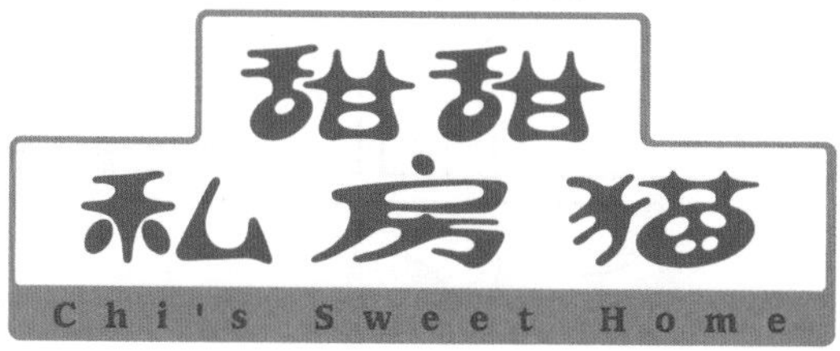

×

Kentucky Fried Chicken

肯德基

Meo-what! Chi was selected as a campaign character for Kentucky Fried Chicken in China!! From December 26, 2011 through January 18, 2012, KFC diners could select between three different combo meals for a chance to collect one of four Chi cell-phone straps. There were even television commercials broadcast. Saying "I want to collect all of them for her but I'm still one short," scores of people made repeat visits, and the campaign was a huge success! Apparently, 5,000,000 straps were made!

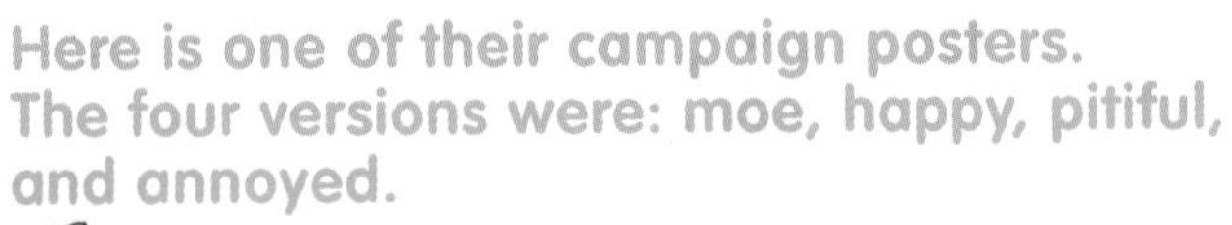

Here is one of their campaign posters.
The four versions were: moe, happy, pitiful, and annoyed.

肯德基
买"喵"招套餐，把小奇带回家！
阳光明媚，快带我出去玩嘛！呜呜~
—怜小奇
肯德基 宅急送 4008-823-823
网上订餐 KFC.com.cn
This is an in-store only backlit display poster.
MRR
DID THEY POST UP THAT FACE IN THEIR STORES?
MEOW
EVEN THE MENU WAS CAT-SHAPED!
买"喵"招套餐
含小奇猫挂饰(一款)
A餐 33元
B餐 33.5元
C餐 34元

And here are the special combo meal boxes!

In Shanghai, many posters were seen in subway station platforms and in bus-stop shelters. At many stores, by the end of the campaign their warehouse was entirely out of the strap toys! To all of Chi's fans in China, we hope you continue to support her! Thanks!

A recently discovered sheet of posted paper reveals an unexpected fact.

Chi's Sweet Home volume 10

ON SALE NOW!!

Chi's Sweet Home, volume 9

Translation - Ed Chavez
Production - Hiroko Mizuno
Tomoe Tsutsumi

Copyright © 2012 Konami Kanata. All rights reserved.
First published in Japan in 2012 by Kodansha, Ltd., Tokyo
Publication for this English edition arranged through Kodansha, Ltd., Tokyo
English language version produced by Vertical, Inc.

Translation provided by Vertical, Inc., 2012
Published by Vertical, Inc., New York

Originally published in Japanese as *Chiizu Suiito Houmu* by Kodansha, Ltd., 2010-2011
Chiizu Suiito Houmu first serialized in *Morning*, Kodansha, Ltd., 2004-

Chi's Sweet Home strap toys: © Konami Kanata · KODANSHA/TV-TOKYO · Chi's Sweet Home Project. All Rights Reserved.

This is a work of fiction.

ISBN: 978-1-935654-42-1

Manufactured in the United States of America

First Edition

Second Printing

Vertical, Inc.
451 Park Avenue South, 7th Floor
New York, NY 10016
www.vertical-inc.com

3 1901 03696 1540

Special thanks to: K. Kitamoto